STEP INTO READING®

STEP 2

DISNEP
PRINCESS

D0110206

Surprise
for a
Princess

By Jennifer Liberts Weinberg

Illustrated by Peter Emslie
and Elisa Marrucchi

Random House  New York

Once upon a time
there was a girl
named Briar Rose.

She lived in
the forest with
three fairies.
Their names were
Flora, Fauna,
and Merryweather.

One day,
the fairies sent
Briar Rose out
to pick berries.

While she was gone,
they planned
a surprise.

"Let's have a party
for Briar Rose,"
said Merryweather.
"With a cake!"
said Fauna.

"And a dress
fit for a princess,"
said Flora.

Flora began

to make the dress.

She cut.

She pinned.

She trimmed.

Merryweather tried
to help.
But the dress
was a mess.

There was too
much cloth.
And there were too
many bows.

"Oh, no!"
said Fauna.
"It is awful!"
said Merryweather.

Fauna began
to make the cake.
She read from
a cookbook.
It said she needed
eggs, flour,
and milk.

Fauna mixed.

And spilled.

And dribbled.

And dropped.

The milk dripped
onto the floor.
And the eggs
rolled off the table!
<u>Crack</u>!

At last the cake
was baked and iced.
But the icing slid
off the top.
And the candles
would not stand up.

"It is awful!"
said Merryweather.
"A flop!"
said Flora.

The fairies began
to worry.
Briar Rose was
coming home soon.

"I know just
the trick,"
said Merryweather.

She gave each fairy
a wand.
"Magic!"
they cried.
With a wave
of their wands . . .

<u>Poof</u>!

The cottage

was clean as

a whistle.

Poof!

The cake

was as pretty

as a picture.

Poof!
The dress
was fit
for a princess.

Briar Rose came home.
"Happy birthday!"
cried the fairies.

"Thank you!"
said Briar Rose.
"This is the
best surprise ever!"

The End